Captured Emotions

TO: Emma & Roman

Phillip S. Joyner

Captured Emotions

~

Phillip S. Joyner

Strong Finish Publishing

Captured Emotions

Copyright © 2007, 2008 by Phillip S. Joyner

Captured Emotions may be ordered through booksellers or by contacting:

Strong Finish Publishing.
P.O. Box 47834
San Antonio, TX 78265
www.Philjoyner.com

Because of the dynamic nature of the Internet, any Web addresses or links contained in this book may have changed since publication and may no longer be valid.

The views expressed in this work are solely those of the author and do not necessarily reflect the views of the publisher, and the publisher hereby disclaims any responsibility for them.

Cover Design: Art1 media Designs

Photo: Tony Leverett

ISBN: 978-1-61658-936-3 (pbk)
Printed in the United States of America

To Rasyne N. Joyner and Jacqulin Joyner.

Dedicated also to Rennea Myree

Contents

ACKNOWLEDGMENTS

Special thanks to Ministers Grady and Juanita Morris for their editorial expertise and encouraging support. A very special thanks to my foster Mother, Ann Williams, the woman who loved me, raised, me, and most importantly introduced me to my Lord and Savior, Jesus Christ.

There are two other special individuals I would like to thank:

Bishop David M. Copeland, my pastor, my teacher, and my mentor, thank you for invitation to come close. It has brought me closer to God and it has helped me to build character.

Pastor Claudette A. Copeland, when others talked to me about going to hell, you taught me how to escape the hell I was living. Everything I was practicing came from hell. Through your inspirational sermons I made up my mind to practice Christianity.

FIRST SIGHT

The first time I saw you was the first time I cried.
I thought about all the things I tried to hide.

Before that moment, the pain was buried deep.
The cost of those tears didn't come cheap.
Oh, the pain that made me weep.

But you were there, my angel sent from above.
You protected me and all the ones I love.

Genesis 50:20

LITTLE MAN

Little man, little man
playing catch me if you can;
hide and go seek
small, innocent and weak.

The time for games is over now.
I'm sorry, you'll just have to wear a frown.

Protect your sister, hug your brothers
remember you no longer have a mother.

I know it's not something that you want to do;
it's a lot for a little boy like you.

As you grow you'll remember the pain and also take some of the blame;
it's not your fault, no need to feel shame.

So, in the future when you start to complain,
remember how far you came.

Philippians 3:13

UPON A TIME IN AN EMPTY TEMPLE

Once upon a time in an empty temple
lived a little boy whose life was simple.

Three square meals a day
and he slept on a cot;
then one day it all stopped.

After that sudden change
his life was forever rearranged.

That simple life was no longer the same;
all the old comforts turned to new pain.

He often dreams about his past
and wonders how long this situation will last.

The feeling of home has long been gone;
how much longer will this pain go on?

DINNER DREAMS

A treat without meat.
A pan of water and something that looks like corn meal
Stir it up, mix it up until the pan is filled.

Stick it in the oven and turn on the light,
then stare at it for the rest of the night.
You need heat to cook not just light.

It's not that bad
when I look at that particular night in the past.
Little children shouldn't play with gas.

Our eyes wide open and full of gleam.
No dinner tonight; it was just another dream.

THE INNOCENT COOK

A small cook innocent and weak,
hunger drove him to cook something to eat.

A pot full of water, and a dash of flour,
he let the pot boil for a couple of hours.

A short term memory left him with little power;
his own life he was about to devour.

The nose of a neighbor smelt the cook's savor;
call 911 was the thought God gave her.

He heard a siren roar before an axe came crashing through the door.
My angel, you were there to protect me once more.

A shield of protection, He's provided me day and night;
that's why I'll serve him the rest of my life.

A TIME WHEN EVERYONE WAS BLIND

I remember a time when everyone around me was blind.
Blind to my needs
despite all my pleads.

Blind to the need to prepare me for the first day of school.
No one bothered to walk me, or teach me the rules.

It was great anxiety
for a child living in an adult society
and no one to stand beside me.

So, the closer I go to my teenage years,
the further away from education I steered.

The life of a hustler became appealing,
so I tried my hand at dealing.

Born cool and for breaking rules,
I started to hang where all the hustlers played pool.

A university of crime,
I was there way before my time.

There were no diplomas to be given there;
it was a life where no one cared.

The rise to the top was quick and the fall was fast and hard,
but at the time it was my trump card.

THE LAND OF GIANTS

Once upon a time in a land of giants,
there lived a young boy who's will was defiant.
He was pushed and shoved
and rarely showed love.

With him they did as they pleased,
no matter how hard he begged for them to leave.

In the land of giants I wasn't alone;
there were other giants not yet full grown.

The wickedness of their world was designed
to destroy boys and girls;
our minds is what they tried to confine.

From one generation to the next,
their wickedness was never checked.

Now, I'm a giant in my own right
and I stand for change day and night.

The struggle for change is very slow;
there's still much that I don't know.
Father, give me strength to grow,
help me to learn the things I need to know.

TO BE A CHILD FOR A LITTLE WHILE

In the middle of cloudy day's filled with lots of pain,
I remember a time before all the shame.

I was learning new things like riding a bike and fixing a flat;
little childhood things like that.

A magic place,
riding in an imaginary race.

A feeling of being a child,
just for a little while.

TO BE A CHILD FOR A LITTLE WHILE

I often wonder how that must feel,
all the joy, no worries lots of thrills.

A steady hand for me to hold;
a place to live where it's not cold.

A form of affection,
love or some kind of direction.

A hug or two wouldn't of been bad;
maybe then I wouldn't of been so sad.

Through all of that I still survived
and I'm happy just to be alive.

It's only through grace that I run this race
because I can never return to that magical place;
where my imagination ran wild,
when I was a child for a little while.

I REMEMBER

I remember the first time I said yes or no.

I remember the first time I decided to stay or go.

I remember the day someone answered my prayers,
before that they just stopped, stared and seem not to care.

I remember the embarrassment that I felt,
because of the neglect that I was dealt.

No one seems to remember but me,
how these things have shaped me.

It makes me angry and sometimes enraged,
that time in my life is a dirty page.

If I could erase it, I would;
but it's written in stone.
I can feel the fire burning deep in my bones.

SCREAMS

If I look at the shame
it won't be hard to find my pain.
My heart's been broken
by many different names.

I can still hear those screams,
high pitched and full of pain.
Separation is its name.

What kind of pain is this?
Now I understand my death wish.

That pain was enough to break me in two.
No human being could help me through.
My God, I'm so thankful for you.

PAINS OF A LITTLE BOY RUN DEEP

His hurts run deep,
but he's told he shouldn't weep,
because when a man cries he's weak.

So, the older he grows
the more he sells his soul.

I'm not saying crying would have made it right,
but it could have saved a few sleepless nights.

The pains of a little boy, they run deep
the price he paid didn't come cheap.

He got hurt
from other peoples dirt and evil works.

If I had my way, I would make them all pay,
but deep in my heart the pain would stay
even if I made them all go away.

THE GREAT I AM

I walk in the impossible,

because the "I am" in me makes it possible.

So, I have no fear of the impossible,

because my, "I am" has already made it possible in my past.

That's why I have no fear of my future.

LORD AND KING

You showed me you're Lord and King;
I see you in everything.

I see you in my pain
as you turn them into gain.

You're a conqueror, a mighty lion;
when I was a child you heard my crying.

The pain of hunger and sudden change,
before my life was rearranged.

You've been my rock, my stone of defense;
when I look back it all makes sense.

You're my Lord and King.
I see you in everything.

I'M YOUNG AND I'M OLD

I'm young and I'm old,
I'm shy and I'm bold.
All because of the traveled road.

Mostly rough, rarely smooth,
I looked like a child who was born to lose.

I remember a time when I was truly naked;
people said there's no way he can make it.

They thought they pinned me, but they couldn't see,
there was something greater in me.

Before I arrived at this earthly place,
it was already determined how I would run this race.

I stand before you alive and well,
a heart for God is how I prevailed.

It's because of that I know this,
you can be whatever your heart can wish.

FAMILY TREE

Lord I can't stand the sight of my tree.
When I look at it, all I see is pain and misery.
Everything I see in them, I can't see in me.

Why so much pain?
Why do I feel so much shame?

I can't stand the sight of my tree;
does it mean I can't stand the sight of me?

Every time I turn around
it's me they're trying to see,
but it's me who hates the tree.
Right now if I have to face the tree,
I would rather not be.
I am desperate for freedom,
Lord, please help me!

You're all I know,
there's nowhere else I can go.
Just writing this letter to you
takes away my feeling of blue.

The ball of anger I felt is starting to shrink;
because of your grace I begin to think.

ONE IN THE SAME

Rejection and pain is one in the same.
It gives me a reason to shift the blame;
because, it's associated with so much pain.

It's from a time that was out of my control.
A curse passed down from times of old.

It was done to them
and that's all they knew;
I promised I wouldn't do the same thing too.

So, I'll dig deep into my soul
in search of that elusive goal.

I'll need the help of the Holy Spirit,
because my fleshly man fears it.

He promises me comfort as I work through the pain.
It's name is rejection and it makes me feel shame.
What angers me most is there's no one to blame.
They're all dead
and I can't remember their names.

All I have to remember them by is in my head.
Those thoughts make my eye's turn burning red.

Results of rejection
from no family connection.

PAIN BEFORE THE GAIN

Lord, they say to know you is gain,
but no one told me about the pain before the gain.
Before you can reach the gain,
you have to dig through pain.

From broken relationships
to broken promises.
It's left a feeling of loneliness inside of me,
a deep hurt that won't let me be.

My past sin's have cost,
my relationship with my brother to be the lost.
I miss him deeply; my spirit mourns within;
I wonder if he feels my spirit with him?

I can't say yes and I can't say no,
but I know he did eighteen years ago.

It's been that long since I did us wrong;
I loved my brother;

he taught me to be hard and strong.
I miss my brother, he's been gone so long.

BROTHER WHERE ART THOU

Last night I dreamed of death,
all night until the next afternoon.
That feeling of separation made me scream so loud
you could hear it in the next room.

Like it was back in the day when it was hard to get out of bed,
even after the word was read.

I prayed all day and night as well;
the feeling of loneliness had me trapped like a prisoner in jail.

My hope is that you're alive and you'll live forever
and that you'll find peace
and that your pain would be released.

I pray that your wandering journey will end,
that you'll find God and let him live within.

The weight you carried as a child was heavy for any man to carry.
You had to hold me when the monsters in the closet would scare me.

I wish you were here with me as our past I try to bury,
because my monsters still come out to scare me.

THE CROSS

In the cross lost souls are regained
and there's healing for your shame.
If I love the cross there's nothing to lose
and everything to gain.

In the cross there is no mistakes, no risk;
wherever your heart is broken he'll fix.
The cross means everything to me.

In the cross there's answers to all your questions and desires.
When you are down he'll take you higher,
give you strength and power,
to make it another hour.

FREEDOM DIVING

Freedom diving is what I do.
It's what happens when I search for you.

A search for truth, to find who I am.
It's a quest to be a Godly man.

I can't be free to change in this earthly trod,
if I'm not honest with myself
and honest with God.

Freedom diving is what I do,
because it brings me closer to you.

It opens the way to my heart,
breaks it and mends it back together again.
When it's all done living can begin.

The closer I get to you the more love I see.
Freedom diving has done this for me.

A tool of healing
for all my hurt and broken feelings.

A WORD

I'm in the fight of my life and I don't know exactly what to do.
So I do only what I know to do.

Pray for a Word from you, at night till dawn;
until then I press on.

Send it through scripture

send through a friend

or when I use my pin.

A Word Lord just send.

JOY

Lord, thank you for bringing joy into my heart today.

That's your way of letting me know,

That everything is going to be okay.

ANOTHER VALLEY

One day I cried and had thoughts of suicide, but why?
When for my soul Christ already died.

No more need for dope;
in him is how I cope.

He's where I go through life's valleys,
homeless in my car parked in an alley.

In my search for acceptance
I knew in him there is no rejection.
He embraces me with love and affection.

YOUR TIME

Your time,
not mine.
I'm here because you allow me to be.

As I look back
there were a lot of things that I lacked.

The reality is, I should have been dead and gone.
It was your time that carried me along.

My life is not mine, but yours,
so I'll accept the pain I endured.

Some may think it's a horrible story,
but I say, to God be the glory.

So when it's time,
it's time until then;
I'll just press forward
because it's not mine, not now nor has it ever been.

So not one day will I miss time with you,
because one day without you
is a day of frustration and a feeling of blue.

When I depended on things of the world,
I went to the world.

Now, on you I depend,
so time with you I'll spend.

ALONE IN MY CLOSET

Alone in my closet where no one can see,
Lord I feel your presence there with me.

Just like an eagle soaring in the sky
a feeling of freedom passes by.
It's your spirit that I can't deny;
that's what I need to get me by.

Even in my pain, I see reason's for joy.
Lord, keep me in your arms forever more.
The feeling of freedom
I cherish and adore;
just like that eagle my heart begins to soar,
like a mother holding her baby boy.

Alone in my closet, there's no feeling of pain;
your loving spirit always remains the same.
From the beginning of time to the end of mine
your spirit inside me will always shine.

Because your landing is full of joy,
I'm protected in your spirit forever more.

When I walk in my own grander, as I often do,
you show me your ways I should pursue.

Alone in my closet instructions I receive,
visions of worry's passing I see.

What kind of love is this you have for me?

RED EYE

All I saw was red,
when I looked inside of my head.

Today, yesterday, and probably tomorrow.
All of my life I can recall sadness and sorrow.

Yesterday's pain,
today's anguish,
tomorrow's sorrows,
I need to find some other emotions to borrow.

How about forgiveness,
gratitude, or love,
all beautiful gifts from above.

SHAKEY GROUND

Once I walked on shaky ground,
no love in my heart;
only anger could be found.

Now, the ground I walk on is firm,
supported by God's words of wisdom,
love and grace.
Now, the anger from my heart He has erased.

THE WELL

The well of life is deep,
full and never runs dry.
You can draw from it's goodness
until the day you die.

There's a well in each of you
preparing you for God's kingdom, it's true.

The first draw is heavy to pull.
As time goes on it's lighter,
but the bucket is just as full.

The Lord knows how to lighten your load,
and continue to do so as you grow old.

MY PEN, MY FRIEND

My pen, my friend.
You help me dig deep within;
before the tape recorder and TV shows like *Law and Order,*
you were used to write God's order.

You're the instrument no one ever thinks of,
but you were there to record the record of love.

You were used to document the crucifixion of my Lord
my savior, my friend.

You are great and powerful in the right hands;
you're a life saver for this man.

Whenever I'm in trouble and I don't know why,
I pick you up and sort through any distorted lie
or picture of deceit.
It's my faith the devil tries to defeat.

You've shown yourself mighty to me in my defense.
My pen, I lean on you like a friend.

PRECIOUS GIFTS

Compassion, wisdom and love,
all precious gifts from above.

Foundations you laid
the price you already paid.

Teach me these gifts so I can savor,
teach me how to love my neighbor.

On the other side of the table is where I need to be.
Take the beam out of my eye so I can see
compassion, wisdom and love,
things available from above.

GRAVE CONNECTION

I've always felt connected to the grave,
because I couldn't trust the living.
You showed me a love
that will never stop giving.

I was bound by anger, loneliness and fear,
in this new day I feel you near.

You give me victory over death and the feeling of doom,
when I couldn't go further you showed there was room
to receive love from above.

You suffered on the cross for me when my soul was lost.
You showed me I could hate my past and look forward to things to come.
You showed me that my life was far from done.

LIFE AND DEATH

I was once connected to a dead past, bound by fear.
You freed my spirit; your voice I now hear.

I looked forward to death, because I didn't know life.
All the time inside, the enemy was planting the seed of suicide.

Now, I have a vision of a future that is mine.
A place where the sun shines,
where there's no place for gloom.
I've finally shut the door to that room.

YOUR DESTINY, MY DESTINY

Born righteous and full of grace, with all power in your hand,
you took the form of a humble man.

Because you hung yourself on the tree,
from the troubles of my mind I'm finally free.

Apart from you I am nothing, but if I remain in you,
you'll show me all my fears and comfort me too.

Then a journey with a true friend can begin
where hope springs through again.

HEART VS MIND

Lord, in my heart I want to do your will,
but in my mind I want to kill.

I want to be an ambassador and represent your nation,
but I'm bound by my past frustration.

Sanctify me, renew my mind
that I may see your face when it is time.

COUNTLESS PEBBLES

My pains are like pebbles on a beach, countless.
A number that could never be reached by human sight.

Then came your love, so pure and true;
all my life I searched for you.

If I die, I'm not afraid;
if I live I'll follow the path you've paved.

THE WAYS YOU MOVE

You move in two ways, big and small;
I've learned to appreciate them all.

You move at two different times that's day and night,
whenever you think the time is right.

When I look back over my life, I see the ways you moved;
it was just about the time I thought I was going to lose.

TAKE ME TO THE RIVER

Knowing yourself on the surface will get you nothing
but deep observation; through meditation
you will gain great revelation.

Things you thought you faced and put behind
will reappear and take a front place in your mind.

The root of pain and suffering runs continually like water
from the falls
that pours into a lake which leads to the river's wall.

The river is the place I seek.
That's the place where the motions are calm
and the boat barely rocks; no leaks.

A place where the visuals are serene
and the sounds are peaceful.

No roaring from the falls, no over spills from the lake;
anything happening is suppose to take place.

It's hard to find but possible to have last.
That's what I deal with when I look at my past.

ENTITLEMENT

I did something wrong and it bothers me so;
the spirit of poverty won't let me go.

It's a fear my needs won't be met;
it brings on stress and it's hard to rest.

It has a hold of me; I can't break free.
It's got me like a man dangling from a tree.

My mind goes back to where it all began;
it leads me back to that little man.

He's too afraid to ask, too young to have cash.
I reverted back to my childhood in just one flash.

A time when I whispered my words low and sweet,
when they ask me if I had anything to eat.

No, not today,
and I can't remember if I did yesterday.

It was the day I stole that pie;
they asked me if I did it and I told a lie.

BEFORE IT CAME

When I weep, you weep, because you understand my pain.
You knew it was on the way before it came.

On the cross, you bore that and more;
it will all be for your glory when you reveal what's in store.

For the tears I've shed I have no shame,
because you understand from whence they came.

IN MY WEAKNESS

In my weakness, I'll live for you.
In my weakness you're my strength and my light, it's true.

When my load is heavy, you are my support.
When vengeance and hate fill my heart,
you take the pain and set it apart.

In my weakness, those thoughts I can't control.
In my weakness, you comfort my soul.

LONELY HEART

Lonely heart
where do I start
or when will you be finished with me?

Someday soon I hope and pray
that these emotions will fade away.

Like the change in seasons
you come and go for different reasons.

You're like a shadow that follows me wherever I go,
and my every move you know.

Oh lonely heart, what is it you seek,
is it you, mother, is it you brother?
If not, then Lord, you're the other.

Fill this hole that's so deep,
fill this hole so I won't weep.
Most of all, fill this hole so, I can sleep.

MY FIRST AND ONLY WAY

Teach me, Lord, where I keep going wrong;
discipline me and make me strong.

Those things I put before you, you've taken them all away.
Now, I turn to you, my first and only way.

So here I am; me, myself and the great I am.
It's time I learned your original plan.

It's not about things in my pocket that ring ching-a-ling.
You desire to hear my heart sing.

You are Lord, and there is no one above.
Then I will be ready to receive true love.

THANK YOU LORD

Lord, thank you for love, peace, and joy.
You continue to lavish your love on me;
undeserving of it as I am,
you give it generously.

Because of your love,
I know who I am.

I'm your son who strays from time to time
and acts just like I've lost my mind.

A DESIRE VS. AN EMOTION

Between lust and loneliness
I have only found sin.

A desire verses an emotion,
it starts with a look and notion;
together it's a deadly potion.

LUST

Lust won't let me rest.
Lust, if I follow you,
I'll have to repent and confess.
Lust, I realize that your are just a test.

Lust wants to make me a slave.
Lust, if I let you,
you'll send me to an early grave.

FOR MY SOUL'S SAKE

I fiend for your love
like an addict for drugs;
you've unlocked the mysteries of life from above.

When I accepted your love from the start,
you planted a seed in the pit of my heart.
As time goes on it continues to grow,
but there are still things I don't know.

Missing love from my birth,
I'll have to do some work that might hurt.

Lord, keep my mind on this journey I'm about to take,
I'm only doing it for my soul's sake.

THE BATTLE

In my mind, there's so much of you;
in my action there's so much of me.
The battle rages on tremendously.

Seems like the more I seek you
the more of me rises up.
I try to resist, but my appetite for sin
gets stronger and stronger deep within.

The closer I get to the crime
the more I back away.
This seesaw battle must end today.

My flesh wants it, but my spirit says no;
I get confused and don't know which way to go.
In the end no matter which way the wind blows
sorrow closes in and grips my soul.

SWEET COMMUNION

Lord, thank you for restoring my hope and increasing my faith.
I wait patiently for Communion with you through grace.

For a time I couldn't feel you near,
but just like you promised, your presence has reappeared.

A BOX WITH NO NAME

A box of pain with no name,
still I count it all gain.

There was a time when I couldn't say that,
because of where I was, but this is where I'm at.

As the day's go on
it's easier to look back on all those things that are worn and torn.

For every new day that is born,
all I think about is watching you perform;
new acts of healing,
as I discover what's in this box of feelings.

I'M DONE

I've done all I can and did all I can do;
Now, Lord, I guess I'll turn it over to you.

I know I've said it a time or two before;
now that I've messed up, I'll say it once more.

The world is yours and everything in it;
I'll just have to remember my day is like your minute.

So, Lord, my life is yours; use me as you please;
to understand what that is I'll have to spend more time on my knees.

That means less TV and less of me,
more of the word
and less gossip about what I've heard.

Lord, you're wonderful and marvelous;
it takes patience to put up with all my mess.

With all my anger and all my rage,
you've still allowed me to watch my mother age.

She knew it and you did too,
it's going to take a lot of prayer to bring me through.

WHEN

When will I ever be free?
Every day there's new pain and less joy for me.

Although old sadness has passed, remorse of future pain remains.
I could run fast and far from my problems, but they wouldn't change.

I would only get tired and find the same person who
I was running from right there too.

DAY AND NIGHT

I search for you day and night;
sometimes it's really hard to fight,
but I keep pushing because it feels right,
for at the end of the tunnel I know there's light.

My lack of understanding sometimes brings fear,
so you stir me inside and your voice I can hear.
Sometimes in words, sometimes through sight,
that's why I seek you day and night.

LIFE

You stole my soul and crushed my spirit;
when I saw something I wanted you wouldn't let me near it.

When I stood up, you beat me down
and on my face there's a constant frown.

My friends say "smile" so I try for awhile,
but my spirit has been torn and my soul is worn.
That's why my face has taken this form.

So don't think I'm mean;
think about the things I've seen.
I've seen children neglected,
abandoned and rejected,
left alone
with no place to call home.

My friends say "smile," I try for a while,
but the pain within
takes away my grin.

THE PLOT

Your plot against me started before my existence.
Your evil has always been persistent.

You've pierced my flesh and staggered my emotions,
but today I have tasted the joy of the Lord's potion.

Now hope is restored; there's a new generation to teach.
I have new goals to reach.

My hope gives way to new ideas and new opportunities exist.
This is a whole lot better than that awful wish--
a wish of death and non-existence,
your plot you carried out with great persistence.

THE CIRCLE

I find it, I lost it,
sometimes I refuse it.

The circle of loss
I can no longer pay the cost.

Rescue me I pray;
pull me from the circle today.

Make my way straight and give my heart joy,
a feeling I've never known, not even as a boy.

How I survived I don't understand.
Please, Lord, reveal to me your plan.

The circle is no longer just inside me;
now even other people can see.

If others see the pain I feel,
the time must be here for me to heal.

Show me the way out of the circle today.
Show me the way I came, Lord, I pray.

LORD, IT'S BROKEN AGAIN

Lord, it's broken again,
a lost love, another lost friend;
but I still have your love on which I can depend.

You're closer than my brother; better than a friend;
you're with me I know, till the end.

It's broken again, not in one place but a few,
but I can't quit because you're in me, and I'm in you,
and my desire to love is true.

It's broken again,
but you're still there, my Lord, my Savior, my friend.

Wherever I go, I'll let the world know
that you're a friend even when their hearts are broken.

BLESSED

I have been blessed
more times than I can confess.

By your grace I'm carried
as I watched my friends being buried.

My life, I don't take for granted;
people around me don't understand it.

You've blessed me with insight and understanding;

when my life became demanding I leaned on you, and you keep me standing.

There were times when I stumbled and failed,
but because of grace I still prevailed.

So, if you look at my life and shake your head,
stop, thank God for grace instead.

The road I traveled God only knows;
where it will end has not yet been told.

So, as I wait for it to be revealed,
I'll be fine if I stay in his will.

CHRISTMAS PASSED

I looked at a picture today,
a memory that will never fade away.
A happy time, a happy place;
thanks for the love that special day.

Before we met,
that day I would always regret.

But now, from year to year,
that day I will no longer fear.

The anger has been released;
now in my soul I feel peace.

SUFFERING AND MOVING

Suffering and moving is a thing of my past;
no longer does the pain have to last.

I'm free to move without suffering loss;
it should be painless without a hidden cost.

So why does my will fight with me to move;
why the fear that I might lose?

The ability to stay put some take for granted;
not being able to do it sends me into panic.

Why must I suffer this life in pain;
maybe if I share, my living won't be in vain?

SEE YOURSELF

One day I beat myself,
because I hated myself, for loving myself.

How could I love myself,
because I knew myself?

Until one day I decided to love myself,
then I decided to change myself.

I discovered I had a choice about self.
Then I realized what I was taught about myself;
that's why I was a danger to myself.

So, to love yourself
is to see yourself;
to see yourself
is to change yourself
according to how you see yourself;
then you can be yourself.

A little knowledge is a little power,
but a little knowledge beats no power.

So find the time
to free your mind,
or you will find
yourself left behind.

FINALLY FREE

Thank you, Lord, for my peace
and all the anger that's been released.

Once I lived to hate; now I live to love to
for that Lord, I thank you.

I'm finally free
to be myself
and who created me to be.

You've opened a window to wisdom,
the door to love and understanding.
the book of life, patience, and compassion.

My future is in these pages too
that turn daily as I learn to walk with you.

Now, you are a part of my life every day,
and this is what I say each day,
when I make time to pray:

Lord, walk with me today like you did yesterday.
Make your presence known all through my bones,
then I'll let these words be known.

If I consistently seek you,
I will consistently find you;
for that Lord, I thank you.

LORD LIFT ME UP

Lord, lift me up;
my spirit is down but
there's nothing in my mind
that I can find.

Take me to that place where the waters are still and the grass is green,
and teach me what these feelings mean.

You are my rock; your hands are unchanging
and your love is amazing.

I've worshipped many things in life,
but when I held them too tight they cut me like a knife.

Lord, to you I now cling;
Finally, songs of joy my heart can sing.
Melodies from heaven
release the tears I've held since I was seven.

SEPARATION

The day will come when you'll have to say good-bye.
You'll be strong and try not to cry
and remember that we are all born to die.

Life's been good; life's been great.
You loved hard and tried not to hate.

Like all good things, you must come to an end;
while you were here you tried to win.

Despite your loss and what that cost,
without His guidance your soul would be lost.

You loved and lived the life you loved,
and one day your spirit must go up above.

GLORY TO YOU

I was strong until I was weak.
I was content in my loneliness
until I tried love and lost.

I stood strong in anger
until I could find no one to hate.

In all these things I was ashamed,
until I gave glory to your name.

Until I brought glory to you,
my old way's hindered my breakthrough.

Now that I'm wiser and older,
I will let you take the hurt off my shoulders.

I offer it up to you as a sacrifice
and move on with my life.

If for some reason it rises within.
I will offer it up once again.

ISBN: 978-1-61658-936-3
Printed in the United States of America